BREAK THE CODE

THE CONTEST

00:00:04

BREAK THE CODE

Megan Atwood

darbycreek

MINNEAPOLIS

Darby Creek
A division of Lerner Publishing Group, Inc.
241 First Avenue North
Minneapolis, MN 55401 USA

For reading levels and more information, look up this title at
www.lernerbooks.com.

The images in this book are used with the permission of: © iStockphoto.com/
TomFullum (teen); © Andycash/Dreamstime.com (digital clock); © Vidakovic/
Bigstock.com (Abstract technology background); © iStockphoto.com/archibald1221
(circle background): © freesoulproduction/Shutterstock.com (game pieces).

Main body text set in Janson Text LT Std 12/17.5.
Typeface provided by Adobe Systems.

Library of Congress Cataloging-in-Publication Data

The Cataloging-in-Publication Data for *Break the Code* is on file at the Library of Congress.
ISBN 978-1-4677-7509-0 (lib. bdg.)
ISBN 978-1-4677-8104-6 (pbk.)
ISBN 978-1-4677-8834-2 (EB pdf)

Manufactured in the United States of America
1 – SB – 12/31/15

To my parents, always.

CHAPTER 1

"You're one of our most promising students, Maiv. What made you cheat?" The principal looked over her glasses and stared hard at Maiv.

"I didn't cheat, Ms. Jackson. I promise, I didn't." Maiv felt tears in her eyes but kept her voice firm. "And I can't believe you'd trust an anonymous note more than me."

"It's not the note that convinced me. It's the answer key we found in your locker."

Maiv forced down her rage. She had to stay calm. She had to be reasonable. Sure, an answer key for a recent test didn't look good. But she *hadn't* cheated and never *planned* to cheat, and her best bet was to stick to the truth. "I didn't put it there."

"If you can explain how that answer key got in your locker without you putting it there, I'm listening."

But of course Maiv couldn't explain. She knew who was to blame, but she couldn't tell the principal.

The Benefactor had framed her.

"I don't know how it got there. Someone else must've found out my locker combination."

"Any idea who that would be?"

Maiv took a deep breath. She hadn't shared her locker combination with anyone. And she wouldn't lie about that. She wouldn't frame someone else for this. "No. But how would I even get my hands on an answer key in the first place?"

"You tell me, Maiv. Your computer science teacher says you're her brightest student. It wouldn't surprise either of us if you were able to hack into her computer and copy that document from her files."

"But if I *am* her brightest student, why would I need to cheat?"

The principal sighed. "I'm sorry to say I've seen it happen before. This is a big disappointment, Maiv. But since it's your first offense, we won't put you on academic probation. You'll receive a failing grade on that test—"

"But that'll lower my GPA!" For the first time, Maiv panicked. She was counting on her grades to get her into college—and to get her the financial aid and scholarships she would need.

"Consider yourself lucky," said the principal. "I'm cutting you a break here. I'll be calling your parents to let them know about this."

Maiv swallowed back more protests and just nodded. Her parents would be horrified. Maiv never got into trouble. How would she face them tonight?

Because she couldn't tell them about the Contest either. She couldn't tell anyone.

As soon as she left the principal's office, she sprinted to the nearest bathroom, locked herself in a stall, and let herself cry.

But not for long. She had work to do.

* * * * *

Entering the Contest had seemed like a good idea at the time. Maiv's family desperately needed money. Her father was on medical leave for foot surgery, and that meant a big pay cut. Her mom worked three jobs, and each one killed her back. Maiv hated watching her wince through household chores, so she ended up doing all the housework when she could. She didn't get to be oblivious like her five younger siblings did.

Plus, Maiv really wanted to go to college. But that couldn't happen without money.

So last week, when she got an email from someone called the Benefactor, offering her a chance to join a contest with a $10 million prize, she'd jumped at the chance. To win, she just had to complete ten tasks ahead of three other contestants. Maiv loved games. And she never lost.

Except this one, it seemed.

She'd found out fast—scary fast—that the Benefactor wasn't hosting this contest for fun or out of kindness. The money had just been bait to get her on board. She was being used, manipulated—*trapped* into following the Benefactor's orders. And now that she was part of the Contest, she was in it for better or for worse until the bitter end.

Her first task had been strange, but easy enough: write an article about teen runaways for the school newspaper. Maiv was the paper's editor in chief, so she had no trouble getting the piece published. Still, it made her uncomfortable.

But that was nothing compared to the second task. Yesterday, the Benefactor had asked her to create a computer virus. The kind of virus that could wipe out all the information on a computer's hard drive. They didn't *say* that it was a virus or what it was for, but Maiv could tell from the instructions. Maiv still couldn't decide what creeped her out more: the fact that the Benefactor wanted her to do this or the fact that he knew she *could* do it.

Maiv wanted to be an engineer—a software engineer. She'd done a lot of research on viruses, hoping that someday she could design antivirus software to protect computers.

Instead, she'd had to create something that would damage a computer. Just the thought made her sick to her stomach.

She'd tried to refuse. She'd tried to quit the Contest. But the Benefactor wouldn't let her. So Maiv had done as she was told: created the virus, placed it on a flash drive, and sent the flash drive to an address in South Minneapolis.

And then she'd gotten down to the real work.

Maiv was a good student, a good daughter. She went to church and worked hard and took care of her family.

And she hacked.

As she'd learned more about coding and systems, she'd discovered hacking almost by accident. And it had become her secret hobby: sneaking past firewalls, decoding encryptions, taking peeks at information no one was supposed to see.

It was just for fun. For the challenge. She never changed or used anything. It wasn't like she was stealing people's social security numbers. Maiv had no interest in hurting anybody or in breaking the law. But the hacking gave her a sense of control, a feeling that she could solve any problem, find a way around any barrier.

Except when it came to the Contest. Maiv couldn't find a way to hack the website. She'd tried for hours last night and had gotten nowhere. Which made her wonder several things.

One: how was she ever going to find out anything about the Benefactor if they had covered their tracks so well?

And two: why had the Benefactor asked her to create a virus when they were clearly capable of doing it themselves?

Then she'd gotten her second email from the Benefactor.

> Your actions are a violation of the Contest rules. You will be punished.

And now she *had* been punished. Maiv had no doubt that the Benefactor had somehow arranged this cheating accusation. They'd probably do something even worse if they caught her breaking the Contest's rules again.

If they caught her.

CHAPTER 2

From the start, Maiv had known she was being watched. The Benefactor knew too much about her, about her family. And it hadn't taken her long to find the bugs.

There was a tiny camera in her locker, disguised as a magnet. And a listening device behind her desk lamp at home. She'd pretended not to notice them. Because this meant the Benefactor, or someone working for the Benefactor, had been in her house, in her school, without leaving any other trace. No broken locks, nothing out of place. And if they could do that once, they could do it again. Maiv didn't dare remove the bugs, for fear that they'd be replaced—and that she'd be punished.

And that might not be the only way the Benefactor was monitoring her. She was pretty sure someone had installed a keystroke logger on her computer, tracking everything she typed. Maiv changed her computer password once a month, but her antispyware program was out of date. Even if she found and removed the keylogger, the Benefactor might just invade her home again and reinstall it.

She was also pretty sure she was being followed. She kept seeing the same middle-age white guy lurking near her usual bus stop before school. He'd never been there before. On some level, that creeped her out more than anything else.

Still, she had no intention of letting this Benefactor win. Whoever they were, they had intruded on her privacy, ruined her chances for a scholarship, and blackmailed her. So for Maiv, that meant one thing: war.

If there was one thing she'd figured out from her brief and creepy interactions with the

Benefactor, it was that there was a master plan somewhere. A master plan with wiggle room to take care of any glitches that might come up.

Standing by her bugged locker, she made a decision. She'd figure out what that master plan was. And then she'd find a way to ruin it.

In history class, Maiv pretended to be taking notes. Instead, she scribbled down what she knew about the Contest so far. With the Benefactor monitoring her digitally, old-school paper and pencil seemed like the best way to keep track of her thoughts.

Benefactor has contestants threaten one another, send items to one another, so there's no trail back to the Benefactor. And so that there is a trail back to us. We're being framed for the Benefactor's actions.

If they can bug our homes, computers, and phones, they can also probably erase the evidence. Scrub our emails, delete the website. Make it look as if none of this ever existed. The only evidence left would be what we've done. Our fingerprints on items. Our faces caught on public cameras.

Why is the Benefactor going to all this trouble? What is the purpose?

Why did the Benefactor choose me? Why were the other contestants chosen?

Are the other contestants competing because they want to? Or because the Benefactor is forcing them?

The other contestants must have answers to at least some of these questions. Of course, first she'd have to figure out who they all were. And then find a way to talk to them—without the Benefactor knowing.

Maybe if she created an entirely new email address, from a computer the Benefactor couldn't possibly expect her to use . . . Maiv thought up a new name and wrote it down This would be the email she'd use to talk to the other players.

Once she found them.

For now, she would pretend she'd learned her lesson. She would let the Benefactor think she was following the rules.

And she would see where this Contest led her next.

CHAPTER 3

Between classes, Maiv checked the Contest's
website for her third task. She was supposed
to buy a burner cell phone and hoodie and
sweatpants—guy sizes. Then she needed to
program a single phone number into the phone.
The phone number was listed on the website—a
St. Paul area code. Finally, she needed to mail
all these items to James Trudeleau in East St.
Paul by 8:30 tonight.

So: good news and bad news. The bad news
was that she was going to be even busier than
usual after school. The good news was that she
had another contestant's name. If she could

find a safe way to make contact with this James Trudeleau, maybe they could work together.

Right after school, Maiv went into the nearest phone store and bought the cheapest prepaid phone in the place. Next, she stopped at the thrift store and picked up the clothes, spending the last of her meager babysitting money. Had the Benefactor even considered that she may not have enough money? She had no way of getting hold of them if she came up short. Maybe she could just say out loud, "I need money for this task," and one of the many listening devices would pick it up. She almost snorted out loud at the thought. The Benefactor had dangled $10 million in front of her nose, and yet the Contest had made her even poorer than she already was.

In line at the checkout, she glanced at the time. Already almost four. She had to hurry home to meet her sisters at their bus stop. That meant she wouldn't have time to mail these items. She'd have to do it later tonight, after dinner. It would be hard to get out of the house once she was home, but she'd just have to think of something.

When Maiv came out of the store, she saw her bus closing its doors. She sprinted, the plastic bag with the clothes thwacking against her knee. Just as the bus began to pull away, Maiv reached it and banged on the door. The bus driver frowned and stopped, then opened the door.

"You're lucky, missy," she said and then lurched the bus forward right after Maiv got on. Maiv stumbled down the aisle and found an empty seat, wiping sweat off her temple. Close call. Her sisters would have had no one to meet them and walk them home. And she would have been in a ton of trouble.

Especially because Adam's family was coming to dinner tonight.

Adam was in Maiv's grade, and their parents had been friends for years. Maiv knew Adam liked her—he was so obvious sometimes it hurt. And Maiv's mom, especially, thought Adam was a great catch. He was Hmong. He was from Laos, like them. And he was a really good guy.

Maiv knew her parents would be perfectly happy if she got married—to Adam—right after high school. But that wasn't going to happen. Adam was sweet, but she just wasn't interested. Still, she needed to help her mom with dinner and tidy up the house before Adam's family showed up.

Meanwhile, Maiv took out the burner phone and got it activated. She plugged in the number she'd memorized from the Contest's website. Then, tugging nervously at her hair, she glanced around the bus. No one seemed to be paying any attention to her. She was pretty sure none of these other passengers were Benefactor spies.

On impulse, she hit the call button.

She could get in trouble for this, big time. But since she'd just bought this phone, the Benefactor couldn't be bugging it.

"Hello?" A man's voice. "Who is this?"

Maiv hadn't really expected an answer. What should she say? Was she talking to the Benefactor?

"OK," said the man, "I know it's you, whoever you are. Listen, I've done everything you asked. I've told you everything you wanted to know. When can I be done with this? I know you have things on me, but—I can't keep doing this forever. EarthWatch was a good place to work . . . Hello? Are you there?"

Maiv frantically tried to process what she was hearing. Definitely not the Benefactor. Another contestant?

The man swore under his breath and then hung up.

Maiv took a deep breath. This had to be another person being blackmailed by the Benefactor. She called back, but this time there was no answer. A voicemail message kicked in: "Hi, this is Paul. I can't answer my phone right now, but leave a message . . ."

Maiv opened her mouth to speak, and then she realized—if the Benefactor was bugging this guy's own phone, the Benefactor would hear her message. And punish her.

She hung up. She couldn't risk it.

Not yet, anyway.

CHAPTER 4

At the bus stop, Maiv picked up her sisters:
ten-year-old Kiab and five-year-old Lili. Lili
bounced off the bus holding a large piece
of paper.

"Look, I drew you!" Maiv looked at the
picture and saw her whole family drawn there.
Her twin brothers, three-year-old Liv and Leev,
her brother Cai, and Kiab and Lili and Maiv
were all standing up, holding hands. Her parents
were drawn lying on beds.

Maiv's heart broke. She knew if her mom and
dad saw that picture, their hearts would break
too. They wanted so badly to be able to do more.

Maiv hugged Lili and said, "That's beautiful, little flower. Maybe you can give that to Niam and Txiv for Christmas?"

Lili nodded, excited. "A present!" She opened her worn backpack and stuffed the picture in. She'd probably forget about the picture in about ten minutes. Maiv made a mental note to take it out of her backpack later tonight.

After she figured out how to finish Task 3.

* * * * *

When Maiv and her sisters walked in the door, their mother shooed the younger girls down the hall. "Go say hello to your father," she told them. Then she turned to Maiv, her eyes worried.

"The principal called—"

"Niam, I didn't cheat," Maiv said in a rush.

"I didn't think you did, honey. I can't imagine you ever doing something like that."

Of course, her mom also couldn't imagine Maiv hacking. Or being stupid enough to get mixed up in something like the Contest.

"This has to be some kind of mistake," her mom went on. "That's what I told the principal. Your father feels the same way."

Maiv nodded gratefully. "Thanks, Niam. I still want to clear my name, but I don't know if I can. I'll talk to my computer science teacher tomorrow and see if I can sort it out with her . . ."

Her voice trailed off as she noticed a thin string around her mother's neck. "Did you go to the shaman?"

Maiv's mom instantly brightened up. Even with six kids, three jobs, and a bad back, her mom was the happiest person Maiv had ever met. "Yes! I think it helped my back. I feel better already."

Though the Mouas were Catholic, they still practiced traditional Hmong rituals and sought help from the shaman. Maiv noticed their family altar had also gotten some additions. Her mom was going all out.

Though Maiv was happy her mom felt better, she knew this would be short-lived. The rituals helped, but Maiv knew that rest, pain relief, and some medical tests would help too. If only doctors weren't so expensive and her mom could afford to take time off from work. If only the money from the Contest were real.

"How's Txiv?" Maiv asked.

"He just got home."

"He worked today? Does that mean his foot is better?"

Maiv's mother gave a little shrug. "He needs to go to the shaman too, but you know how stubborn he is."

Just then, Maiv's dad came into the living room, moving slowly—trying to hide the limp. When he saw Maiv, he grinned, though Maiv could see the pain behind his eyes. "I knew something was missing! Two of my wonderful daughters came home from school, but I could've sworn I had three."

He didn't even mention the cheating accusation. He came over and kissed her forehead like he always did. Her father never let his worries or his doubts show.

Maiv couldn't help asking, "Txiv, should you be going to work with your foot like it is?" It had only been two weeks since the surgery. And the bills were starting to come in. But the healing wasn't happening as fast.

He winked at her. "You don't worry about me. I worry about you! That's my job. My foot can run four hundred miles, right now."

Maiv swallowed down tears. She knew how much her parents wanted her to be just a kid. But she never had been. Not with so many younger siblings to take care of and money tight and always feeling a bit like an outsider, wherever she was.

"We'd better get started on dinner," said her mother. "The Yangs will be here at six."

Maiv nodded. "Be there in a minute."

She ducked into the room she shared with her sisters, found an empty cardboard box Kiab had been saving for an art project, and packaged up the clothes and phone. She'd figure out how to actually mail them later.

In the kitchen, Maiv got to work with her mother and sisters. The four of them formed a line at the table and started making spring rolls for dinner. Maiv loved moments like this. Even with her twin brothers running around like fools and getting in the way.

When the doorbell rang an hour or so later, Maiv's father limped over to open the door. There stood Adam with his parents. While they gave the traditional greeting of asking if they could come in, Adam smiled at Maiv.

"*Koj tuaj los*," her father said, and Maiv smiled back at Adam. He was one of her oldest and closest friends. She wondered if she could ever see him as anything more.

"You start the physics homework yet?" he asked her as he stepped into the living room and took off his shoes. "Mrs. Kildare was *rude* about all the homework this time around . . ."

That was as far as he got before the twins and Lili sprinted toward him. Cai, her thirteen-year-old brother, lifted his head in greeting but then ignored him. Kiab just flopped on the couch and waved. Lili yelled, "Are you Maiv's boyfriend?" Her whole family giggled, especially Kiab. Maiv rolled her eyes. Her siblings.

Maiv's dad swooped Lili up and threw her in the air, her laughs tickling Maiv to the core. Meanwhile Adam started chasing the twins around the tiny house. A minute later Lili joined in, and then Kiab. Even Cai jumped in, grabbing little ones and swinging them around.

Maiv loved the sound of her family laughing more than anything.

And Adam fit in so perfectly . . .

Maiv gave herself a mental shake. This wasn't the time to analyze how she felt about Adam. She had a contest to sabotage.

* * * * *

After dinner, as the Yangs put on their shoes and said good-bye, Maiv checked the time. It was 7:30. There was no way she'd get out of the house now. Not with dishes to do and bathtime for Liv and Leev.

Adam smiled at Maiv, and she had an idea. "Can we talk outside for a minute before you go? About that physics homework?" He nodded, looking so happy Maiv felt a thud of guilt in her chest.

"Great. Give me one second, I'll be right there."

Maiv ran to her room and grabbed the package. Then she slipped on her shoes and sneaked out the back door. Adam was waiting for her.

"Can you do me a favor?" she asked him.

His eyes widened and he nodded. "Sure. What is it?"

She swallowed. "OK, this will seem weird, but I need you to mail this package for me tonight. The FedEx by your house should still be open. The address is already on there, and I'll pay you back for the postage." She handed the box to him.

He looked down at it, eyebrows furrowed. "Uh. Yeah. What for?"

Maiv smiled. "A birthday present. For a friend. But it has to be mailed tonight or it won't get to him in time for his birthday."

Adam's shoulders deflated just a little. "Oh. OK. No problem." Maiv heard the disappointment in his voice—after all, she'd never sent *him* a birthday present. Instantly she felt guilty. Not only was she using him, she was letting him think—but she stopped herself there. Adam could think whatever he wanted. Maiv wasn't his girlfriend, and it wasn't his business if she was seeing someone else.

Still, she hated to hurt his feelings like this.

But she had a hunch she'd be doing far worse things as this contest moved forward.

CHAPTER 5

Half an hour later, Adam texted Maiv to let her know he'd mailed the package. The worry that had bunched up in Maiv's shoulders relaxed a little. Until she remembered that she had seven more tasks to go. And still no idea who was behind this or how she could end it.

In the bedroom she shared with Kiab and Lili, Maiv opened up her super-old laptop. While the younger girls were in the bathroom brushing their teeth, Maiv checked her email.

Asking someone else to help you with a task is a violation of the Contest's rules. You will be punished. Meanwhile, if you complete Task 4 correctly, you can still win the $10 million prize. Check the website for your next task.

Maiv let out a shaky breath. She should've seen this coming. Avoiding the bugs in her house hadn't been enough. Her phone was probably being tracked too, which meant the Benefactor had seen Adam's text. Or worse, someone could've been watching her when she gave Adam the package. The scope of the monitoring felt so intrusive, so scary, that Maiv could hardly breathe. Her whole body trembled and she had to stand up and walk around.

Now she would be punished. Again. She had no idea what the Benefactor would do to her this time. Or if someone else would get hurt. Her family. Adam. Maiv was close to a full-on panic attack.

But then she swallowed down her terror. There was nothing she could do about the punishment now. She would just have to wait and see what happened. Anyway, it was clear that the Benefactor still needed her. She wasn't being kicked out of the Contest. She was just being backed into a corner. Not only could she not quit—she also absolutely could not tell anyone else even a little about what was going on. The Benefactor did *not* want other people involved. Which just confirmed Maiv's suspicion that the Benefactor's master plan was highly shady. But whoever they were, they were determined to guard their secrets well. Only Maiv, the other contestants, the Benefactor would know about the Contest.

Which meant Maiv needed to track down her fellow contestants.

She had the phone number for someone named Paul. And she had two addresses. It wouldn't be hard to find out who owned that phone and who lived at those addresses. Maybe they were contestants, maybe not, but it would be a start.

Except that she couldn't use her own computer for that research. Not if the Benefactor was monitoring it. She'd have to wait until tomorrow, when she could use a computer in the school library.

Meanwhile, she had to keep following the Benefactor's instructions. Maiv grabbed her computer and went to the living room, so that she wouldn't keep her sisters awake. "What are you up to, honey?" asked her mom, who was coming out of the boys' bedroom.

"Just have to finish up a couple of things for the paper, Niam."

Her mom frowned slightly. "All right, just don't stay up too late."

Maiv forced a smile. "I won't. Good night."

Once she was settled on the couch, she pulled up the website.

TASK 3 COMPLETE

TASK 4

3:15

Hack into the Mutual Insurance database and erase any records of Karen and Greg Burnett. You have until midnight.

Maiv shut the computer like she'd been burned.

CHAPTER 6

Maiv took a deep breath and opened her computer again. Best to get this over with. *If you can't beat 'em, join 'em—or at least let 'em think you've joined 'em.*

Maiv found the insurance company and then, using software she'd built herself, found a way into their system.

It took her exactly ten minutes. That's how good she was. And yet the Benefactor was better. Which meant they didn't need her to do this for them. Unless they *wanted* her to get caught.

Scrolling through the policies, she found

Karen and Greg Burnett's file. She scrolled through the policy and saw the word "Deceased" stamped over Mr. Burnett's name.

Karen Burnett was a widow. A widow who was about to lose the record of her insurance.

Maiv had a squirmy feeling in her chest, as if tiny animals were walking around inside her. Tiny, angry, scared animals.

She took a closer look at the policy. The Burnetts owned a hardware store in North Minneapolis. This was a hazard policy—insurance that covered the store in case of fire, water damage, hail, theft . . .

So, if she deleted this record, the Burnett business would have no safety net. It would be as if they'd never had insurance at all. Any damage to their store would have to be paid for out of their own pockets.

She inhaled sharply. How could she possibly do this to someone?

Maiv got up and paced. She chewed on her lip, then her thumb. She did about five laps in her room. Finally, she deleted the file.

"I'll find a way to fix this," she whispered

to the screen, as if she were talking directly to Karen Burnett. "I promise."

* * * * *

TASK 4 COMPLETE

Check back tomorrow morning at 7 a.m. for your next task.

Maiv was about to shut down her laptop when she saw that she had a Facebook message. That was unusual. Maiv didn't use Facebook much, and neither did her few close friends.

The message was from someone named "Ima Contestant." Maiv's stomach flipped. Obviously—too obviously—this was a fake name.

But the message itself was gibberish: *I hope you are having a pleasant day. May your days be filled with good deeds. A lot of time has passed since we've met. No words have passed between us. A good code is hard to find.*

A tiny bit of time can feel like eons. Remember, OK? Err on the side of kindness. Yell loud when the mood strikes. Otherwise, what's it all for? Understand the bigger game. It's a tragedy, isn't it?

Not that you don't know that. Thank you for timing things right. Help is a four-letter word. Everyone knows that. Count your blessings, though. Only the strong survive. Now everyone has to play their part. Tell it on the mountain. Eat good food. Sing in the shower. Trace it back to its source.

This seemed like one of those web robots that gathered sayings and stuck them all together. Maiv was about to close the message, but something stopped her. Certain phrases stood out—seemed to be directed to her. "A good code is hard to find…" "Understand the bigger game." Even "help is four-letter word."

She read the rest of the message.

Welcome, friend. Establish that life isn't fair. So what? Haven't you heard? Only the lonely have it bad. Understanding that takes time. Let's consider the options. Don't rush it! Try to see clearly. All things start at the beginning. Life moves on. Kiss the sky and put it all together.

"Put it all together." Could this actually be a coded message?

The words were actual words, so it wasn't a substitution code. Clearly not a numbers code.

Something easy had to be happening here, though. With a name like "Ima Contestant," this person wasn't trying to be too sneaky.

Maiv stared at the message until her eyes blurred. And then it came to her: The first letter of each sentence. When she wrote it down and put it all together, she got:

I'm Ana. Are you in the Contest? We should talk.

Maiv swallowed. Right now, the risk of answering was too great. The Benefactor could find out, especially since this code was pretty easy to break. Then they might punish both Maiv and Ana.

She could try responding tomorrow, from a school computer. And she'd have to create a fake account just like Ana had, since the Benefactor probably already had access to her Facebook account.

It was worth a try. For the first time in a while, Maiv felt like smiling. At least she wasn't alone in this.

CHAPTER 7

The next morning before school, Maiv dutifully checked the Contest's website again.

TASK 5

9:00

Write the following note by hand: "Do not displease us again. Or it will be the last nail in your coffin." Deliver it to the boy working at Burnett Hardware in North Minneapolis by 4 p.m. today. Do not let the boy see you deliver it. Do not speak to the boy. Leave immediately after dropping off the note.

Suddenly it dawned on Maiv. She and the

other contestants weren't just working toward some hazy goal that she didn't understand. They were also working against each other. The Benefactor was using each contestant to keep the others in line. If someone refused to do a task or tried to quit, the Benefactor created a new task for another contestant. A task that was designed to frighten, threaten, or punish the person who had resisted. Someone had planted that answer key in Maiv's locker. And now she had to deliver a threat to the fourth contestant.

It couldn't have been a less convenient task. It would take her forever to get from her school in East St. Paul to this hardware store in North Minneapolis. And then forever to get back. She couldn't possibly be home in time unless she skipped class, and with the cheating accusation so fresh, that seemed like a bad idea. She'd have to think up an excuse to be home late. Her parents knew she stayed late on Tuesday and Thursday to work on the school newspaper, but today was Wednesday . . . Then Maiv had an idea.

Maiv's mother had already left for work, so she and her dad got breakfast for the younger kids. As Maiv poured milk into Lili's cereal bowl, she said, "Uh, Txiv, I'm going to be home a little late tonight. I told Father Michael I'd help out with the after-school program at Sacred Heart."

Her dad sounded shocked and pleased at the same time. "My goodness! What a lovely thing to do, Maiv. I'm so happy you're helping out Father Michael!"

Maiv tried not to let guilt show in her smile.

"My angel Maiv. I am always so proud of you."

Maiv swallowed down tears.

* * * * *

During study hall, Maiv went to the library computers and got to work. First she created a new email account. Then she made a fake Facebook profile. And then she searched for "Ima Contestant."

But nothing came up in the list of possible contacts. Frustrated, Maiv logged on to her real Facebook account and opened the message from Ana. She clicked to view Ima Contestant's profile—and got nothing. The account didn't exist.

At least it didn't exist anymore.

Maiv chewed on her lower lip. The Benefactor must've somehow shut down Ana's secret profile. Maybe Ana had used her real email address to make it. Or maybe she'd been working on a computer that the Benefactor was monitoring. Either way, Maiv had missed her chance to connect with Ana.

That was probably for the best, though. If Maiv had responded, the Benefactor would've known—and had another reason to punish her. For now, she would just work with the information she had.

So far she had Ana's name and the phone number for a guy named Paul. Plus some addresses. There was the place in South Minneapolis where she'd sent the jump drive with the virus. And there was the place in St. Paul where she was supposed to send the clothes and phone last night.

With a little digging, she had some answers.

A reverse phone lookup traced the number she'd called on the burner phone. A guy named Paul Grayson owned the phone. Paul Grayson was easy to find on Facebook. Like a lot of middle-age people, he seemed not to realize that privacy settings existed. His profile said that he had worked for something called EarthWatch, a St. Paul business, until two months ago. He listed his current employment as "freelance." Based on the photos and statuses, he had a wife, two adorable kids, and a huge house. Maiv had a gut feeling he wasn't one of the four contestants. Someone like this—a professional, responsible middle-age guy—would never buy into the Contest. Of course, the Benefactor was clearly blackmailing him. But the Benefactor could be blackmailing a *lot* of people. That didn't mean those people could help Maiv. The four contestants would at least know what she was going through. They would probably be in the same position she was. They were her best bet right now.

The Minneapolis mansion belonged to Philip and Yvette Davenport. Mr. Davenport was a big-time lawyer with a lot of important-sounding clients. Maiv took a shot in the dark. She typed the Davenports' names into the search bar along with the only other contestant's name she knew: *Ana*.

The first hit was a magazine article—a small piece in the "Gala" section. A picture showed two fancy-looking white people—the Davenports, according to the photo's caption. And next to them stood two Latina girls, one about Maiv's age and the other a little younger than Kiab. The caption named them: Ana and Isabel Rivera.

The article's headline said, *Philanthropists Expand Generosity to Their Home*. The article went on to explain that Ana and Isabel were foster children living with the Davenports.

Aha, thought Maiv. *So Ana's not rich. Her foster parents are. But that doesn't mean she's happy where she's at. She must have a reason for wanting $10 million.* Just like she must've had a reason for contacting Maiv last night. Maybe she and Ana were in the same boat—in over their heads.

Since Ana was her age, Maiv started to wonder if all the contestants were teens. That would narrow down the search.

To see who was renting the St. Paul

apartment, Maiv had to hack into the rental company's records. Hacking on a public computer was risky, but by now, Maiv didn't care one bit. And nothing was as risky as letting the Benefactor track her.

The apartment was being rented by Robert Trudeleau. He'd lived there for eight years and had always paid his rent on time. A little more digging showed her that Robert Trudeleau was a widower—his wife had died fifteen years ago. He had a daughter, Beth Trudeleau, who was a doctor and worked for an overseas medical charity, Doctors Together. And he'd had a son, Jack, who was dead. Jack and his wife had been killed in a car accident eight years ago. But *they* had a son—James—who was Maiv's age. James Trudeleau. There he was.

Based on the apartment's location, Maiv guessed James went to her school, Cleveland High. She hacked the school's records—easy enough. She'd done that plenty of times. And there he was: a senior like her. An A student. No record of getting into trouble with the school administration. Maiv pulled out the tiny reporter's notebook she always carried in her purse and jotted down James's class schedule. Maybe she could catch him in a part of the school where the Benefactor hadn't planted cameras.

And now there was Burnett Hardware.

Step one: a basic Internet search. This brought up some general information about the business, which had been around for almost twenty years. The online reviews were glowing. Customers mentioned that the store was family-owned and most said the service was excellent. Maiv did find a handful of negative reviews, though. One said, *Never going back there. The owner's sons work there, and the older one creeps me out.*

Maiv didn't know what the customer meant by that. But she did have a good idea of who she might be threatening now. The Benefactor was probably targeting one of the Burnett sons.

Step two: a more targeted Internet search. The Burnetts seemed to own and live in the apartment above the store. And the high school closest to the hardware store was Alexus Olsen High School.

Step two: hacking. Maiv had never tried to beat Olsen's system before, but she figured it couldn't be much tougher than Cleveland High's security. And it would be faster than searching for other types of records.

She was right. It only took her a few minutes to get past the firewall. And she quickly found what she was looking for. Someone named Colin Burnett was a junior at Olsen.

She didn't have time to find out more because the bell rang. Her study hall period was over.

But she was fairly certain she would be meeting Colin later today.

CHAPTER 8

Maiv was now positive she was being followed. The middle-age white guy she kept seeing at her bus stop was actually on the bus with her now, a few rows ahead of her. He was already sitting there when she got on, and he did a double take as she walked past him. Recognizing her. When she got off the bus, so did he.

He waited at the bus stop while she kept walking. But a few minutes later, she stopped and pretended to look at a store window. Out of the corner of her eye she saw him, about a block behind her.

This went on for a while. Every time Maiv

stopped, her shadow stopped suddenly too and pretended to look at whatever he was in front of.

Definitely not a professional.

Which didn't make it any less scary. Maiv found herself practically running to the hardware store.

It was a cute, inviting store. In the front window an old-school paper sign said, "Yes, we're open" in sprawling script. Maiv opened the door, and a little bell sounded.

A burly, kind-of-cute guy about her age stood behind the counter. He had a tired-looking face. Obviously, this was her fellow contestant.

"Hey there. Can I help you?"

Maiv flinched. She wasn't supposed to talk to him. But it would be weird if she didn't respond to a direct question. "Uh, no. I'm just looking for . . . a hammer." She knew she didn't sound convincing. But it was the first thing that popped into her head. Probably because of the note's wording: *the last nail in your coffin.*

The guy looked at her suspiciously. She

didn't blame him. "Second aisle from the back, about halfway down."

"Thanks."

The phone rang behind the register.

She moved toward the back, figuring she'd leave the note when he wasn't looking.

He called, "Let me know if you need anything else."

Maiv noticed the mirrors on the ceiling and figured he could still see her. So she headed to the hammer section, picked up a hammer, and pretended to look at it. Maybe she should actually buy it and then put the note on the counter while the guy was ringing up the purchase . . .

She moved back toward the front of the store, and then she saw him: the guy who'd been following her, standing outside and looking through the store window.

Suddenly, she felt mad. Mad that this guy had the nerve to follow her. She met his eyes and lifted up the hammer like she was going to throw it through the window at him.

The man's eyes widened, and he backed up fast. A moment later he had ducked out of sight.

Maiv would have laughed if the situation hadn't been so weird.

But then she remembered the guy at the counter. He was still on the phone, his back turned.

Quickly, Maiv took out the note she'd written. Suddenly she felt a strong urge to get out of here. No time to buy anything or even put the hammer back. She just placed the note on the counter and put the hammer on top of it. Then she walked out the door, hoping no strange men were waiting to ambush her.

Maiv had never run so fast to a bus stop in her life.

CHAPTER 9

When Maiv got home, she knew right away
something was wrong. About twenty people
stood around her house and she saw a police car
without its lights on. Her mother was holding
Liv, Cai held Leev, and Kiab held Lili's hand.
Her dad talked to a police officer and Adam's
father. Adam stood near them and listened in.

Her whole family was crying.

This had to be something to do with the
Benefactor.

When she reached her mom, Liv held
his hands out to her so she took him. "Niam,
what happened?"

Wiping her eyes, she took a deep breath and tucked some hair behind Maiv's ear.

"Someone cut through our plumbing system, honey. The whole basement is flooded."

Maiv stared at her. "*Cut* through the plumbing?"

Her mother nodded. "Yes. The police think it might be a hate crime. They can't think of any other reason someone would do this."

Maiv closed her eyes and put her hand to her forehead. Well, it was a type of hate crime. Hate from someone called the Benefactor. Liv started squirming, so she set him down and he ran to Cai.

"Do they have any idea who did it?"

"One of the neighbors thinks she saw a girl with dark hair. But it's Helen, and you know how her eyesight is."

Maiv chewed on her thumb and tried to push the panic down. That had to be Ana. This was Maiv's punishment for having Adam help her. And also a reminder that she had to stay in the Contest. Her eyes filled with tears. This was all her fault.

Her mother put her arms around her, but Maiv had the urge to pull away. She didn't deserve this love. She'd brought this trouble home.

She wiped her eyes. "Will insurance cover this?"

Her mom said, "Your father thinks so. But it will take months to get that money. So we have to clean up the basement before the mold sets in. The electricity will have to be shut off while we work, and we won't be able to use the bathroom for a few hours . . ." She pasted a smile. "But no need to worry. Adam's family will take the little ones for tonight. We called the church and Father Michael is coming over in a bit with a sump pump. We'll clean this up right away."

Maiv stiffened. Father Michael. Now what was she going to do?

Adam came over. He stood awkwardly by Maiv and her mom drifted away, leaving the two standing there alone.

He said, "I'm so sorry, Maiv. Do you have any idea who did this?"

Maiv's eyes filled again, and she looked down. When she looked up, she saw that Adam's eyes were full of concern. This made the tears spill over.

Adam took out a bandana from his pocket. "Uh, here. Sorry. It's all I have. But it's clean. I carry one around in case I decide to play some pickup basketball." He looked down at his shoes as Maiv took it. She couldn't help but smile.

She said, "I didn't know you played basketball."

He grinned. "Not very well. But it doesn't matter. I like it."

Maiv smiled back, but then Adam's expression turned serious. "Listen, Maiv. I know something's going on here and of course you don't have to tell me anything. But, uh . . . I just want you to know that if you need anything or if I can help, I totally will."

Maiv desperately wanted to tell him everything. She wanted to tell someone, just so she didn't have to carry around this weight. But even if she wasn't deathly afraid of the Benefactor and what he'd do, the shame of her involvement was enough to keep her quiet. But right there in that moment, she had a respect and love for Adam that she'd never had before.

"Thank you, Adam. That means a lot to me." The two shared a look and something zinged through Maiv.

And just then, she saw Father Michael pull up.

CHAPTER 10

"Uh, hold on," Maiv said to Adam and the
sprinted across the street to where Father
Michael had parked. He was older than her
mom and dad. Maybe even older than her
grandparents, who were still in Laos. But he had
a spring in his step, and Maiv always though
the twinkle in his eye made him look younger.
She loved Father Michael. He had always
been welcoming to the Hmong community.
The other parishioners said that it was Father
Michael's idea to have a Mass in a dialect of
Hmong. The older Hmong members of the
church always said he had done a lot to make

them feel part of the local Catholic community.

She was running so fast that she almost plowed right into him. "Well, I'll be, Maiv Moua, if you didn't just almost give me a heart attack."

Maiv was too stressed to smile. "Um, Father Michael, today I told my mom and dad that I helped you with the after-school program."

Father Michael leaned against his car and eyed Maiv. The guilt made her stomach squirm. This look was the worst look he could give her. Disappointed and a little confused. He expected better of her.

"And I suppose you're not going to tell me why you said that, eh?"

Maiv gave her head the smallest possible shake. "I—can't. I'm sorry."

Father Michael sighed. "Well, I'll tell you this. I'm not going to lie for you, that's for sure. But I'm not going to rat you out either. So there are two things you have to do for me in return, OK?"

Maiv nodded so hard it hurt. She couldn't believe how great he was being.

"One: you should absolutely help me with the after-school programs. Say, for a month?"

Maiv bit her lip. A month was a long time. Her parents needed her at home, and she'd have schoolwork and hopefully college applications to do too. But Father Michael was being more than fair to her. She nodded.

"Good. We can start that next week, then. The second thing is this: It's not like you, Maiv, to lie about things. So I'm going to assume you have a very good reason for it. But that also makes me believe something isn't right. So I want you to promise me you'll call me if you feel like you're in trouble. Do you promise?" He stared at her with his piercing blue eyes. She imagined he could make anybody want to confess, just with those eyes. But behind the sternness was real love and concern. And this more than anything made Maiv want to cry again. But she nodded and said in a small voice, "I promise."

"Double good. Now help me with this sump pump. We have a house to clean up."

* * * * *

The damage to the basement was extensive. Years of mementos and paperwork were ruined. Still,

Father Michael stayed almost through the whole night helping the Moua family. So did most of their neighbors. Maiv was reminded of how lucky she and her family were.

As Maiv worked, she found a small slip of paper stuck to the wall. Something was scribbled on one side of it. An email address? Maybe Ana had left this for her. Maiv put the paper in her pocket. She could try to contact Ana tomorrow, using the school computers . . . if she didn't get into any more trouble first.

". . . so glad to hear that Maiv is helping you with the after school program," said Txiv to Father Michael.

All Father Michael said was, "Maiv is a good girl. And she's agreed to help all next month!" Then he winked at her.

By the end of the night, Maiv was exhausted and relieved. She and Cai and her parents finally went to their beds around 4:00 a.m. She said to her mom sleepily, "You should call in sick and sleep tomorrow." Her mom smiled at her—the smile that said "how cute."

Of course Niam couldn't call in. They

needed the money more than ever now.

Her mother kissed her on the forehead. "I'll call in for you and Cai, darling. You can stay in and sleep. I'll leave a message now."

And for the millionth time since the Contest had begun, Maiv felt guilt wash over her. But she didn't argue.

Instead, she went to her room and checked the Contest's website.

TASK 5 COMPLETE

TASK 6

2:57

You will receive an envelope. Deliver this envelope to the home of Colin Burnett no later than 7 a.m. Thursday morning.

Colin again. Maiv closed her eyes and prayed this wasn't yet another threat.

Not to mention her bus pass was running on empty. She hoped she had enough coins to stretch it.

And it was already Thursday morning. It looked as if she wasn't going to get any sleep tonight after all.

CHAPTER 11

On the plus side, by this time the morning buses would be running. On the downside, her mom would be up before Maiv got back from her trip. Niam usually peeked into the kids' rooms to check on them before she went to work. If she did, she'd notice Maiv was missing.

Maiv hardly ever locked her bedroom door. For one thing, Kiab and Lili were usually here. She was lucky that the girls were spending the night with Adam's family.

After locking the door, Maiv grabbed her purse and climbed out her bedroom window. Then she circled around to the front of the house and found the envelope sitting on the front step.

Task 6, coming right up.

* * * * *

On the bus, Maiv carefully opened the envelope. Inside she found a driver's license and a credit card, both for Colin Burnett. And a typed note: *Colin: Check the website for your next task. Only use the credit card and ID as instructed.*

Maiv let out a frustrated snort. The Benefactor was using her as a delivery girl. They could've just dropped the note off at Colin's place instead of hers. But they were making her trek to a different city at four in the morning so that her fingerprints would be on this envelope. Maiv felt as though she was a piece in one of those Rube Goldberg machines—the crazy setups that performed a simple task, like cracking an egg, in the most complicated way possible.

She just wished she knew what the egg was. And who had built this awful machine called the Contest.

As Maiv put the cards back in the envelope,

she had an idea. Pulling a pen from her purse, she wrote a message on the inside of the envelope. *Meet me tonight at 8:00 in the Minneapolis Central Library. 1st Floor. Nonfiction, Me–Ne.* She signed it, *Hammer Girl.*

* * * * *

Maiv crept around to the back of the hardware store, thinking she'd leave the envelope at the back door. But when she saw the bike leaning against the wall, with a backpack sitting next to it, she had a better idea. She slipped the envelope into the backpack.

Please see the note, she thought. This might be her only shot to meet up with Colin. After all, she was already more than halfway through her tasks. Time was running out.

* * * * *

Maiv tried not to fall asleep on the long bus ride back to St. Paul. She sneaked back in through her bedroom window, unlocked her door, and fell into bed. By the time her dad was awake and shuffling around, he'd find her snoring away.

And he'd have no reason to be suspicious.

When Maiv woke up around two in the afternoon, she checked the Contest website right away.

TASK 6 COMPLETE

TASK 7

0:45

Write the following note by hand: "You have been punished. We trust you will do the right thing next time." Address the note to "James" and put it in locker 782 by the end of the school day. The combination is 05-23-45.

Maiv sighed. This meant she had to get dressed and head to school. She'd tell her dad she needed work on the school newspaper.

She was starting to get used to this lying thing.

Maiv wrote out the note, folded it up, and wrote JAMES across the back. Then she flipped it over and leaned forward so that her long hair fell in front of her like a curtain.

Maybe that would screen her hand from any Benefactor cameras. She wrote the same message she'd written to Colin, except that she signed it "A friend."

Take that, Benefactor.

CHAPTER 12

That night, getting out of the house to go to the Minneapolis public library was easier than she expected. Maiv rushed through dishes and kid bath time and told her parents she had to go study at a friend's house. Her parents didn't even question her. The guilt about lying seemed to be lessening. Maiv didn't think that was a good thing.

After three bus transfers, Maiv got to the library at 7:55. And by 8:05, she and Colin Burnett were sitting across from each other in a locked, windowless study room.

For the first time, Maiv really looked at him. She hadn't gotten a good chance when she'd visited the store. His eyes had dark circles under them, and he kept clenching and unclenching his fists. His expression was a cross between terrified and hopeful, which was exactly how Maiv felt.

She remembered how she'd erased his family's insurance. She almost asked him if everything was OK with the store, but she couldn't bring herself to. There would be time for that later.

"Who are you?" Colin demanded.

"My name is Maiv Moua. I'm working for the Benefactor—just like you, and Ana Rivera, and James Trudeleau."

James hadn't shown up. Maiv figured he hadn't seen her message on the back of the threatening note. But at least she and James went to the same school. She could find him tomorrow if she really needed to.

"You seem to know a lot about the situation," said Colin, eyeing her suspiciously.

Maiv knew he had no reason to trust her yet. But she still bristled at his tone. "I'm finding out as much as I can. But the Benefactor is a bit . . . shy."

Colin grunted in amusement. "Yeah, that's one way of phrasing it."

"And meanwhile, they're putting us at risk. And our families."

Colin nodded, but he still looked tense. "Why did you agree to do this contest?"

Maiv gave him the short version of her family's financial problems and her own dilemma about college. "But the Benefactor isn't interested in helping us."

"Right," said Colin. He seemed on board now, ready to talk. "They're interested in using us to do their dirty work and then framing us for whatever it is. And it's scaring the crap out of me at this point. They've threatened my family, and my latest task was to buy a gun. I'm supposed to deliver it to Ana by Saturday night."

Maiv nodded, trying to look calm. So now there was a gun. If she'd had any doubts that they were in real danger, those doubts were gone. "We need to put an end to this before someone gets hurt."

"I'm with you there," said Colin. "I was hoping it would help to figure out what the endgame is. Why they're doing all this. It has to be part of a master plan."

"I think so too. I just haven't been able to figure out what that plan is."

"Well, one of my tasks was to go to SolarStar, and someone there mentioned Huffman Industries. So I've been looking into that . . ."

Maiv blinked. "SolarStar? Huffmann Industries? I haven't heard of either of these places."

"They're businesses. I think they're working together on some kind of top-secret project, and someone wants that project to fail. Someone connected to Huffmann Industries, I'm guessing. See, a while back, Huffmann Industries was about to partner with an oil company, but that deal fell through. Instead Huffmann Industries teamed up with SolarStar, which does environmental stuff—way different from what the oil company was doing. I figure a bunch of people involved with Huffmann Industries were like, 'Dude, that's not what we want. We want to drill for oil, not—make solar power or whatever.' You know?"

"And you think someone was mad enough to

try to sabotage the new partnership?"

"Yeah. The Benefactor wanted to plant a bug in the SolarStar offices. I couldn't pull it off but maybe Ana did. And some sort of important project is in the works with those two companies. Maybe the Benefactor wants to mess with that project."

"And instead of doing it directly, they're having us do it."

"Yeah," said Colin. "We're each doing little pieces of the bigger plan, and eventually—"

"The egg breaks," murmured Maiv.

"Huh?"

She shook her head. "Never mind." Then she smiled at him. "This is great, Colin. Now that I know these businesses are involved, I can hack into their systems and—"

"Whoa, you can *what*?"

"Oh. Yeah." Maiv blushed. "I—I can hack into almost anything. It's—just a hobby. I just like knowing how things work, being able to find my way around a firewall. The challenge of it, you know. I don't ever do anything destructive, like steal information or . . . " She stopped, thinking of the insurance.

"Well, I think that's an awesome skill," said Colin. In a teasing tone, he added, "At least if you're using it to snoop on the Benefactor and not on me."

Maiv took a deep breath. "Colin, I *did* use it on you. I hacked into your insurance company's database and erased the records of your family's insurance."

Colin's face went white.

"It was a task," Maiv added quickly. "The Benefactor told me to do it. I—I felt awful about it. And I didn't realize then that your store was—failing."

"It's not your fault," said Colin. His fists were clenched again, Maiv noticed. "And my mom is getting us a new policy, so I'm sure it'll be fine. Not that it won't be expensive." He tried to slip back into a cheerful tone. "Another reason I really could've used that prize money!"

This time, Maiv managed a small smile. "I'll settle for getting to the bottom of this."

"Deal."

CHAPTER 13

Maiv gave Colin her new secret email address, and he agreed to make one of his own so that they could stay in touch. Then Maiv headed to the library's public computers. Time for some hardcore hacking.

Her first target was SolarStar. It was an engineering firm that worked on green energy projects for businesses. According to SolarStar's definition, green energy was basically anything that wasn't oil or coal. But the company's big focus was on finding new ways to get energy from the sun. Maiv moseyed around SolarStar's firewall to have a look at their database and at the employees' emails. Mostly she looked for references to Huffmann Industries.

And she found them. Over the past six months, the CEO of Huffmann Industries, Corinne Huffmann, had exchanged a lot of emails with SolarStar's deputy director, Len Steinberg. The messages were friendly, casual. But serious business was in the works.

From Corinne: . . . *Let's not discuss the project details over email. I'll give you a call later today* . . .

From Len: . . . *and I speak for everyone here when I say we're thrilled to be starting this journey with you* . . .

From Corinne: . . . *I don't need to tell you that I'm facing some resistance from my people. They had their hearts set on the ChemOil deal. A partnership with you folks just rubs salt in the wound. And my father's not helping. Retired or not, he makes it clear when he doesn't approve of my decisions. And plenty of powerful people in the industry agree with him* . . .

From Len: . . . *We've been working with EarthWatch, an up-and-coming thinktank in St. Paul. You probably remember the name from when Paul Grayson used to work there. The product design will come from them, but we'll vet it carefully before bringing it to you . . .*

From Corinne: . . . *If any details about the project leak out before we have a prototype in the works, we could lose our edge in the market . . .*

Maiv didn't follow most of this, but she got the gist.

Huffmann Industries and SolarStar were planning to work together on a *huge* project. Lots of money was involved. Cutting-edge technology was being developed. And both companies' reputations were on the line.

Maiv sat back at the computer and rubbed her eyes. It was already 9:00. She'd told her parents she'd be home by now. But she just couldn't yet. She had to investigate Huffmann Industries. Based on the emails, it seemed like everyone at SolarStar was excited about the partnership. But the people at Huffmann Industries—not so much. And if this whole contest had been designed just to ruin that partnership . . . then the Benefactor was connected to Huffmann Industries.

Maiv jumped when the loudspeaker

overhead announced that the library would be closing in one hour. She needed to work fast.

Huffmann Industries' security was a fortress. It reminded Maiv of the Contest's website: impossible for her to hack. At least not on such short notice.

In desperation, Maiv went back to regular old Internet searches. She looked up Corinne Huffmann. And then she had an idea.

She looked up someone else who had been mentioned in the emails.

If she hadn't been so exhausted, she would've done a victory dance.

Maiv had what she needed.

CHAPTER 14

When Maiv got home, almost an hour late, her parents were sitting on the couch with grave looks. Maiv swallowed.

"Hi, Niam. Hi, Txiv," she said as she closed the door. Cai, who'd been sitting in the living room with their parents, got up and left, widening his eyes at Maiv before he did. She knew she was in some major, major trouble.

Her mom said in a low, dangerous voice, "Young lady. Where have you been? We've been worried sick."

Maiv looked down. "I'm sorry, Niam. I lost track of time."

Now her father sat forward and clasped his hands. "I think you also ran out of friends. We called everybody we could think of that you could be studying with and no one had seen you."

Maiv's heart dropped to her feet. The look of disappointment on her dad's face nearly killed her.

He shook his head. "Maiv, we trusted you. And you lied to us."

Tears started down her face. "No, Txiv, I didn't! I swear! I was studying. I just went to the library . . ."

Both her parents looked at her with sad faces.

Her mom said, "We trusted you about the cheating issue at school. And now this, Maiv. How can we believe you? This is not the daughter we raised."

And that did it. Maiv burst into tears and ran to her room.

She lay on her bed sobbing. They were right—though not for the reasons they thought. These past few days, she had lied, hacked, and worse. All for money. Her parents would be so disappointed in her if they knew about the Contest. She cried until she couldn't open her eyes anymore. Lili and Kiab cried too. They hated to see their sister cry. But Maiv wouldn't let them hug her. She didn't deserve it.

She finally dried her eyes and patted her sisters back to sleep, kissing each one on the cheek. She fell asleep with tears in on her face. At some point during the night, she felt her mom's soft hand stroke her hair, but she pretended to be asleep. She didn't deserve their forgiveness. She *wasn't* the daughter they'd raised.

* * * * *

Early Friday morning, Maiv woke up feeling awful and good at the same time. She felt awful about her parents and her actions. But she also felt good. Because she remembered all the progress she'd made last night. She'd met Colin. And she had a good idea of who the Benefactor might be.

But that didn't stop the Benefactor from giving her more tasks. Task 8 was to deliver another package to Ana's house. Maiv hoped this would give her a chance to talk to Ana—if she could find Ana and get her away from her camera-filled home.

Maiv got dressed and went to the kitchen to help her mom with breakfast. And to apologize. Before she could say a word, her mom wrapped her in a hug. "You know we love you, right?"

And there the tears were again. She just nodded and said, "I'm so sorry, Niam."

Her dad walked in at that moment and stroked her hair. Then said in a booming voice, "It's time for all kids to wake up!"

Lili came in rubbing her eyes. She said to her dad, "Txiv, you are so loud in the mornings." They all cracked up.

I won't let the Benefactor hurt my family, Maiv vowed. *Or anyone else's family. I won't let that happen.*

CHAPTER 15

For two days, almost nothing at all happened. No one seemed to be home when Maiv dropped off Ana's package. Not that Maiv dared to look very hard. And the Contest website told Maiv to wait until Sunday afternoon before checking for her ninth task.

TASK 8 COMPLETE

Your ninth task is to run away. Leave a note in your handwriting that tells your parents you are leaving. Remember: once you complete this task, you only have one more task to complete before you receive $10 million. If you win, a $5 million check

will be given to your family, and you will
receive the other $5 million where you are.

Tonight, by 12:45 a.m., go to the corner
of Nicollet Mall and Jefferson Avenue.
Find the white van and wait there for your
last task.

Maiv closed her eyes. Her heart broke yet
again. Her first task came back to her now. The
piece for the school newspaper, the article about
teen runaways. About how more and more
teens fell into this category. If she disappeared,
that article would make it seem as if Maiv had
been thinking about this, planning this, for a
long time.

She hadn't planned it, but the Benefactor
had. Which meant Maiv probably wasn't the
only one who would have to run away tonight.
All the contestants must be close to finishing
their ten tasks by now. And once those tasks
were done, the Benefactor wouldn't need them
anymore. So why have them run away and meet
at a white van?

Maiv suddenly felt sick to her stomach.

What do you do with software you don't need anymore? You delete it.

Especially if you don't want to leave a trail.

The contstants were the software.

She needed to talk to Colin. Now. Which meant she needed a laptop. Which meant . . .

Adam.

For once, she didn't need to lie to her parents. She told them she was going to Adam's house, and they were thrilled. So was Adam when she texted him.

When she got to Adam's place, she didn't waste any time. "My laptop's broken. Can I use your computer?"

He said, "Hello to you too!" Maiv laughed nervously. "I mean, sure. I'll go get it. Are you doing a project?"

Maiv lost her smile quickly. "Um. Sort of."

At Adam's kitchen table, on Adam's laptop, she logged in to her fake email. Colin was online, she saw with relief. She wouldn't even have to email him—she could just instant message him. She typed out, *Colin, are you there?*

Adam opened the fridge. "You want

anything to snack on?"

"Um, not right now, thanks."

I just got Task 7, Colin typed back. *It was to pick up a van. A sketchy white van. I'm pretty creeped out.*

Well, that makes sense. Maiv quickly summed up her suspicions, ending with the worst one: *I think the Benefactor is going to have us killed.*

There was a long pause before Colin responded. *That's insane. They'd never get away with killing us!*

Adam sat down at the table across from Maiv, but she kept her eyes on the screen.

Why not? Maiv responded. *No one else knows about the Benefactor. He's scared all of us into not telling anyone. And if our families find notes in our own handwriting, saying we're running away, what other conclusion could they draw? Four kids who have nothing to do with one another—no obvious connection—except that they happen to be runaways. What does that say to you?*

Colin typed, *But they'd check our emails and see that we were connected by this Benefactor dude and the Contest website.*

Maiv sighed in frustration. She heard Adam clear his throat. She looked up and smiled at him but then kept writing. *Don't you think the Benefactor has ways to wipe the emails? They've bugged our homes, our phones, everything. I'm pretty sure they're even having people following us. And they know at least as much about hacking as I do. I'm pretty sure they'll have no trouble erasing any evidence that the Contest ever existed.*

After a long moment, Colin typed, *Then we need to go to the police. Now.*

No way. Do you really think the police would believe two high school kids about something like this? Not without proof. And I mean real proof: proof of who the Benefactor is.

Fair enough. So for now we keep playing along?

Yes. I hate to hurt my parents, but we can't risk making the Benefactor angry until we have enough info to expose him.

She was about to tell Colin what she'd found out about the Benefactor, but she realized that Adam was looking at her with a puzzled, almost sad expression. "Must be an important project," he said quietly.

Maiv grimaced. "Sorry," she said. "I didn't mean to barge in here and take over your laptop and ignore you."

"It all just happened so naturally," said Adam dryly. The sarcasm caught Maiv off guard. Usually he was so earnest and sweet.

"I *am* sorry," she said again. And she meant it. "I know it's not fair." Her voice wavered.

Adam leaned forward, all seriousness again. "Then why don't you tell me what's up? Something's wrong, isn't it? You're looking totally spooked."

Maiv looked down at the computer and whispered, "I can't tell you, Adam."

"Why? I want to help." There was so much concern in his eyes. Maiv wanted to hug him.

Instead she just said, "You *are* helping."

"By mailing a random package for you and letting you use my laptop? I can do more than that. Give me a little credit here."

Maiv reached across the table and put a hand on his arm. "Adam, if you mean that, I *will* ask you for help. Just not now. If I come to you later, do you think you'd still be willing?"

Adam said, "Always."

Warmth rushed through Maiv. So . . . maybe he was a *little* more than a friend. Or had the potential to be.

"I guess I *could* go for a snack," she said, and Adam grinned at her.

* * * * *

Before Maiv left Adam's house, she checked her email again and saw that Colin had left her a message. *I've got my last three tasks. I'm supposed to take the van to Nicollet mall tonight, close to midnight. I have to give James an envelope with instructions for breaking into SolarStar. Then I'm supposed to drive all four of us to the river. It's just like you said.*

Maiv set her jaw. The Benefactor intended to end the Contest—and probably their lives—tonight.

I agree that we have to play along until the last possible minute, Colin's note went on. *But once we're all together in the van, I think we should go rogue. Drive somewhere far away from the river, give the Benefactor the slip, and then come up with a plan to take them down.*

Maiv couldn't have agreed more. They couldn't just escape the Benefactor. Not without leaving their families behind for real, and probably putting them in danger. So they would have to fight back—make sure that the Benefactor couldn't hurt them or anyone else.

Somehow.

A fragment of an idea formed in Maiv's mind.

"Adam," she said, "you know how you offered to help? Well—for starters, I could really use a loan."

CHAPTER 16

Poor Adam. She'd used him and kept him in the dark. But yet again, he came through. He loaned her more than enough money to buy both bus fare and a cheap phone.

Maiv bought a burner phone with thirty minutes of call time. She hoped that would be enough. Anyway, she only had about thirty dollars left now. The imaginary $10 million would come in handy at this point. She had to admit, even with everything else that had happened, the longing for that money hadn't gone away.

She took the bus to downtown Minneapolis,

plotting the whole way. SolarStar was their target. She needed to warn them. But she couldn't risk calling their offices, in case they were bugged. For the same reason, she couldn't go into the offices in person. She'd have to send a messenger.

At Government Plaza, a few blocks away from the SolarStar building, Maiv sat in front of a fountain, took out one of her reporter's notebooks, and wrote out a message to Len Steinberg.

You are being sabotaged. Someone connected to your partner, Huffmann Industries, is trying to ruin your breakthrough. Call this number so that we can explain.

She wrote down the number for her burner phone.

Do not tell anyone about this note. Your life may be in danger if you do. This is extremely important. We want to help.

She folded up the note. On the back, she wrote SolarStar's address and Len Steinberg's name. Now she just needed to get this delivered . . .

A few kids around Cai's age walked past her.

She caught up to them and stood in front of them. "Hey, do you want to make twenty bucks?"

The kid scowled at her but then shrugged. "Sure. But how do you know I just won't take the money?"

Maiv looked him in the eyes. "Because I trust you."

The boy's face turned red. The other two kids snickered and knocked him in the shoulders. But the kid in front of her said, "Depends on what I have to do."

Maiv put the note in his hands. "Deliver this. Right now. Only give it to Len Steinberg—don't let anyone else try to take it, understand?"

The kid nodded. Maiv took out twenty dollars and put that in his hand. She said softly, "My life may depend on this. Don't let me down." The kids walked away, and Maiv hoped this wasn't her dumbest idea yet.

CHAPTER 17

Back home, Maiv waited for Len Steinberg to call her. After a few hours, she stopped holding the burner phone in her hand like a good-luck charm. He might not have gotten the message. He might not have believed what she was saying. Or he might think she was the enemy. But she had to keep hoping he would call at some point.

Meanwhile, she got her bedroom to herself with talk of a killer physics test she needed to study for.

Even though Maiv was wasn't really running away, she knew the pain she would cause her parents was real. So the note she wrote was blotted with real tears. *I love you. I'm sorry for any inconvenience this causes. I have decided that you would be better off without having to worry about me. I'll be fine. Just know that. I'm figuring things out.*

At the bottom of the letter she added, *Talk to Father Michael. He'll understand and can help you.*

To the Benefactor, that would sound innocent. Just a way to comfort her parents. But once her parents talked to Father Michael, they'd know that she was in trouble. That she wasn't just leaving on a whim.

And then she'd find a way to contact them later. After this Contest was finally over.

Maiv wiped her eyes and then grabbed her backpack. She shoved in what she thought she might need: clothes, toiletries, phone charger, paper and pens. She had no idea how long she'd be gone, but she didn't want to make the bag too full. If she had to run, she wouldn't want the weight slowing her down.

As she was packing, she found the scrap of paper balled up in one of her jeans pockets. The jeans had been washed, and the paper was a stuck together. She opened it up gingerly, recognizing the piece of paper she'd crammed in her jeans the night of the flood.

Ana's new email address.

She'd completely forgotten about it.

It was only 7:30. If she could get downtown and to a computer, she could let Ana know they were on the same team.

She took a long look around her room and hoped she'd see it again soon.

But she knew she couldn't come back until she'd solved the problem.

Maiv opened her window and climbed out into the night.

CHAPTER 18

By 12:45, Maiv had gotten downtown, written to Ana, and sat at a coffee shop for hours. Steinberg still hadn't called.

And now it was too late to talk to him. It was time to head to the meeting spot.

Maiv walked briskly down Jefferson toward Nicollet. The street was eerily empty. She passed a guy getting up from a bench and tossing something into the trash, and across the street she thought she saw a figure lurking in a doorway. Otherwise, nobody.

The van was at the corner, as promised. When she opened the door, Colin gave a little shriek of surprise. She stifled a laugh. His nerves must be completely shot at this point—which shouldn't be funny. But he had a very high-pitched scream for such a big guy.

Still, they couldn't be too careful. Maiv was ninety-nine percent sure the van was bugged. Which meant she and Colin couldn't act as if they knew each other. Or the Benefactor would know they'd secretly been in touch.

"I'm Maiv Moua," she said pointedly. "We've never met."

"Uh, Colin." He got it. Maiv smiled again. They *were* practically strangers, but they were in sync. That had to count for something. It was just about the only advantage they had.

* * * * *

Five minutes later, Maiv stood outside the van with Colin and Ana. "So you know who the Benefactor is?" Ana said to Maiv.

Colin stopped fidgeting and stared at Maiv. "Wait, what? You figured it out?"

"I *suspect* I know," said Maiv. "But I need

to see how everything plays out tonight. And then we have to find proof."

"Yeah," said Ana. "Do either of you know what James is doing in there?"

"Stealing some sort of file—a project proposal," Colin told her.

"And I'm guessing that file contains a physical copy of the schematics for that project," said Maiv. "The electronic copies are probably ruined by now."

Colin cut in. "Now you've lost me. What schematics?"

Before Maiv could respond, Ana asked her, "You mean they only have one hard copy and one electronic file? That seems weird."

Maiv shrugged. "This technology is all pretty brand-new and super secret, so I don't think they're sharing it with anyone. Not even over email. Too many security risks."

"Will someone please tell me what's going on?" Colin asked, his voice going up a little.

Ana said, "All we know for sure is that James just walked into SolarStar with a gun and instructions to steal something."

"*He* has a gun?" said Maiv in surprise. Hadn't Colin said he'd sent a gun to Ana? Was this the same gun, or another one?

Before anyone could respond, they all heard it: sirens in the distance.

"That's probably the police."

Maiv was about to say "Obviously," but suddenly Ana was running down the street.

"Ana, wait!" Maiv shouted, but Ana didn't slow down.

"Start the van!" Ana called over her shoulder.

"Should we go after her?" Colin asked.

Maiv's mind felt surprisingly clear. She calculated the risks. "No, then we'll *all* get arrested if the police show up before we can get away. Let's just do what Ana asked—get in the van and wait for them to come back."

"*If* they come back," said Colin.

Maiv didn't want to think about that. She started back toward the van. If only they'd managed to make contact with James earlier. He might not have any idea what he was walking into. She remembered the person she'd walked past on the way to the van: the guy by the bench, throwing something into a garbage can. That was probably him. Throwing away—something . . .

"So who is it? Who's the Benefactor?" Colin pressed.

"I'll tell you my theory when we're all together," Maiv said, reaching for the door handle on her side of the van. What had James thrown away?

"And what about this EarthWatch project thing? Is this the thing that SolarStar and Huffmann Industries are working on together?"

Maiv hardly heard him. *What had James thrown away?* "Wait here," she said, turning on her heel.

"What?! You said we should stay with the van—"

"I just thought of something! Give me two seconds."

Maiv gestured for him to get into the van. He groaned in frustration as she ran off.

CHAPTER 13

Maiv sprinted to the garbage can, hoping no cameras were watching her. Or that if there were cameras, whoever was monitoring them was distracted by something else right now.

She reached the garbage can and looked in.

Right on top: a handgun.

Well done, James, Maiv thought. At least he hadn't broken into a building while carrying a weapon.

But that weapon must have his fingerprints on it now. And if this was the gun Colin had sent to Ana, and Ana had sent it on to James, their prints would be on it too.

They couldn't just leave it here.

Carefully, she picked it out of the receptacle and held it in her hands. She'd never held a gun before. She didn't like it. But then again, she didn't like a lot of things about this Contest.

* * * * *

A moment after she and Colin got in the van, Ana and James appeared, both out of breath. James's eyes were wide and he shook like a leaf. Maiv's heart went out to him.

Once they were all back in the van, Colin drove through the empty downtown, away from the sound of the sirens. He stuck to the speed limit. *Smart*, Maiv thought. If they passed any cop cars patrolling the area, no one would have a reason to stop them.

No one spoke.

Colin was taking them south—away from the river. Once the sirens had faded, Maiv gestured for him to pull over. Colin shot her a confused look, but she made the hand motions again and he nodded. Once he'd found a spot, Maiv got out of the van, and the others followed.

"I thought we were going to make a break for it," said Colin, sounding a little frustrated.

Maiv said, "They probably have a tracker on the van. We won't get far before they realize we're not following instructions. And then they'll come after us. So we need to make some decisions fast."

She glanced from face to face. Ana looked grim. Colin was clenching and unclenching his fists—a sure sign of nerves. And James looked totally confused and just plain terrified.

Maiv spoke as calmly as she could. "They're going to try to kill us tonight. That's their only move now. And if we call the police, we'll just get arrested. No one will believe the Contest is real. So we have to make a choice. Do we try to get away somehow? Or do we go and meet the Benefactor now, on our own terms?"

"What do you mean by *on our own terms*?" asked James.

"I mean we go after him."

"How?" Colin demanded. Maiv could tell he was getting fed up with being left out of the loop, and she felt bad that she hadn't had time to explain more to him.

"Well, I have an idea," she said. "Look, the Benefactor is dangerous. We know that. You don't mastermind something as complicated as this unless you have some real evil in your heart, some need for control. But I think we can take advantage of that. If you guys will trust me, I think we can find a way to prove that he's behind this—and stop him from hurting anyone else. What do you say?"

Ana, Colin, and James all looked at each other. Then Ana said, "I don't know you at all. I don't know what you have in mind. But no way am I letting this Benefactor get the best of me. No way."

Colin nodded. "Same with me."

James took a deep breath. "After the night I've had—the *week* I've had—yeah, I'm open to anything."

Maiv looked at all three of them and nodded. "Then let's take this guy down."

ABOUT THE AUTHOR

Megan Atwood lives and works in Minneapolis, Minnesota, where she teaches creative writing at a local college and the Loft Literary Center. She has an MFA in writing for children and young adults and was a 2009 Artist Initiative grant recipient through the Minnesota State Arts Board. She has been published in literary and academic journals and has the best cat that has ever lived.